This Little Tiger book belongs to:

_____

_____

To Lucy and Nina ~ M A

For Mom Lynne, Peter Dad and andibles
too numerous to mention xx ~ L S

LITTLE TIGER PRESS
1 The Coda Centre
189 Munster Road
London SW6 6AW
www.littletiger.co.uk

First published in Great Britain 2013

Text by Mara Alperin
Text copyright © Little Tiger Press 2013
Illustrations copyright © Loretta Schauer 2013

Loretta Schauer has asserted her right to be
identified as the illustrator of this work under
the Copyright, Designs and Patents Act, 1988

A CIP catalogue record for this book is
available from the British Library

Printed in China • LTP/1400/0755/0713

1 2 3 4 5 6 7 8 9 10

Little Red Riding Hood

Mara Alperin

Illustrated by Loretta Schauer

LITTLE TIGER PRESS
London

Once there was a little girl who loved to wear red. She had red shirts and red skirts, red shoes and a fabulous bright red cloak. Her name was Little Red Riding Hood.

Early one morning, Little Red's mother
packed up a basket.

"I have a very special job for you," she
told Little Red. "Granny is feeling poorly –
will you take her this fresh fruit?"

"Of course!" cried Little Red, and
she put on her favourite cloak and
kissed her mother goodbye.

It was a bright, sunny day, and Little Red skipped through the woods.

"Good morning!" she called to the rabbits and the deer. "I'm bringing Granny a special surprise!"

But someone was peeping
from behind a tree . . .

. . . A big, hungry wolf!

"Good day," growled the wolf.
"What are you doing in
the woods all alone?"

"I'm taking this special basket of fruit to Granny!" Little Red replied.

"Yuck," thought the wolf. He didn't like fruit. *He* liked to eat tasty little girls!

So the wolf thought up a plan – a horrible, clever plan!

"Why not pick Granny some lovely flowers?" he said.

"Good idea!" said Little Red. But as she started gathering daisies, the wolf raced down the path towards Granny's house.

The wolf knocked on Granny's door with
a **thud! thud! thud!**

"Is that you, Little Red, my dear?" called Granny.

"Yes!" squeaked the wolf. "Let me in – it's
breakfast time!"

"Oh goody," said Granny, opening the door. "What are we having for breakfast?"

"**YOU!**" cried the wolf . . .

"Aaargh!" yelled Granny. "*You're* not Little Red!"
And she slammed the door, right on
his big, furry nose.

"Ow ow ooooowwwwww!"

howled the wolf.

Quick as a flash, Granny
ran out of the back door
and into the woods to
find help.

"Horrid old Granny," the wolf growled, rubbing his nose.

But now he could put his terrible plan into action . . .

So when Little Red knocked
tap! tap! tap! on Granny's
door, it was a deep, scratchy
voice that answered,

"Come in, my dear."

Little Red walked into Granny's
bedroom and stopped in surprise.
"Why Granny!" she said slowly.
"What BIG EARS you have!"

"The better to hear you with, my dear," croaked the wolf.

"And Granny," Little Red said carefully, "what BIG, HAIRY ARMS you have!"

"The better to hug you with, my dear," growled the wolf.

"But Granny," Little Red whispered, "what big TEETH you have!"

And he pounced at Little Red . . .

Just at that moment, the door burst open.
In rushed Granny, with the woodcutter.
"Stop right there!" yelled Granny.

"Put her down now!" bellowed the woodcutter, "or we'll chop you up and turn you into a birdhouse!"

With a terrified howl, the wolf jumped out of the window and ran far, far away, never to return.

Little Red hugged Granny tight. "I'm SO glad you chased that wolf away!" she said. And she gave Granny the basket of fruit.

"What a day of excitement!" laughed Granny. "Now let's all have breakfast!"

Collect every one!

My First Fairy Tales are familiar, fun and friendly stories – with a marvellously modern twist!

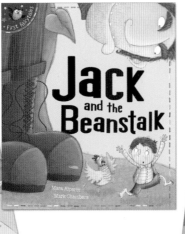

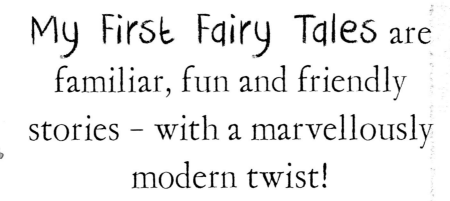

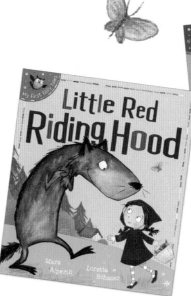

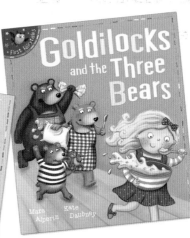

The Three Little Pigs

The Gingerbread Man

Chicken Licken

Rumpelstiltskin

Pssst! coming soon!